# The Things I **Love** About
# Pets

## Trace Moroney

The Five Mile Press

I **love** my pets,
I *especially* love my dog Poppy,
and these are the things
I love most . . .

her kind, sparkly eyes,

her waggy little tail,

and a great big
lick
. . . that says I love you!

I spend lots of time with Poppy,
and these are some of the things
we like to do together . . .

play with a ball,

share an ice-cream,

dig holes,

and, going on adventures
to far-away places!

Having a pet in our family teaches me
how to look after someone else.
I show Poppy that I love her and care
for her by giving her the things she
*needs* every day, like . . .

fresh water to drink,

good doggy-food to eat,

a warm, comfy bed,

toys to play with,

a walk, and . . .

. . . lots of love and attention
and playtime!

But . . . there are some things I have to do
that aren't so much fun — like . . .

explaining to Mum how one
of her favourite shoes
got chewed up,

and cleaning up
doggy-poo!

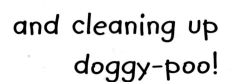

Learning how to take care of my pet
is a fun way to learn how their
body works . . . and how to keep
them healthy and happy.

in

out

Poppy is like my best friend and she
makes me feel happy and loved.

Sometimes, though, if I am feeling sad or
lonely – Poppy just seems to *know* how I feel.
She snuggles up to me and I hug her . . .
which makes me feel much *better!*

Once a year my school has a **Pet Day**.
On this special day we are allowed to
bring our favourite pet to school.
It is *so* much fun . . . and really interesting
to see other pets.

Some are warm and fluffy, some are
slimy and cold, and others are
hairy and scary!

But to me, I think I have the bestest pet in the whole-wide-world!

I **love** you, Poppy.

# Notes for Parents and Caregivers

'The Things I Love' series shares simple examples of creating **positive thinking** about everyday situations our children experience.

A positive attitude is simply the inclination to generally be in an optimistic, hopeful state of mind. Thinking positively is not about being unrealistic. Positive thinkers recognise that bad things can happen to pessimists and optimists alike – however, it is the positive thinkers who *choose* to focus on the hope and opportunity available within every situation.

Researchers of positive psychology have found that people with positive attitudes are more creative, tolerant, generous, constructive, successful and open to new ideas and new experiences than those with a negative attitude. Positive thinkers are happier, healthier, live longer, experience more satisfying relationships, and have a greater capacity for love and joy.

I have used the word **love** numerous times throughout each book, as I think it best describes the *feeling* of living in an optimistic and hopeful state of mind, and it is a simple but powerful word that is used to emphasise our positive thoughts about people, things, situations and experiences.

# Pets

As most pet-owners will agree, owning and caring for a pet is a rewarding and enriching experience, and can have a positive affect on our psychological and physiological wellbeing.

Our pets provide us with companionship, loyalty, friendship, love and affection, and help alleviate feelings of loneliness, stress and anxiety.

Children benefit enormously from having a pet in the family. Valuable life lessons are developed as children learn about responsibility, nurturing, life and death, and – most importantly – ***empathy***.

Trace Moroney

♥

*For Poppy . . .*
*If I were a cat and I had two rats —*
*I'd give one to you.*

Dare to Love

The Five Mile Press Pty Ltd
1 Centre Road, Scoresby
Victoria 3179 Australia
www.fivemile.com.au
Illustrations and text copyright © Trace Moroney, 2011
All rights reserved
www.tracemoroney.com
First published 2011
Printed in China 5 4 3
National Library of Australia Cataloguing-in-Publication entry
Moroney, Trace
The things I love about pets / Trace Moroney.
1st ed.
9781742487113 (hbk.)
9781742487106 (pbk.)
For pre-school age.
Pets--Juvenile literature.
636.0887